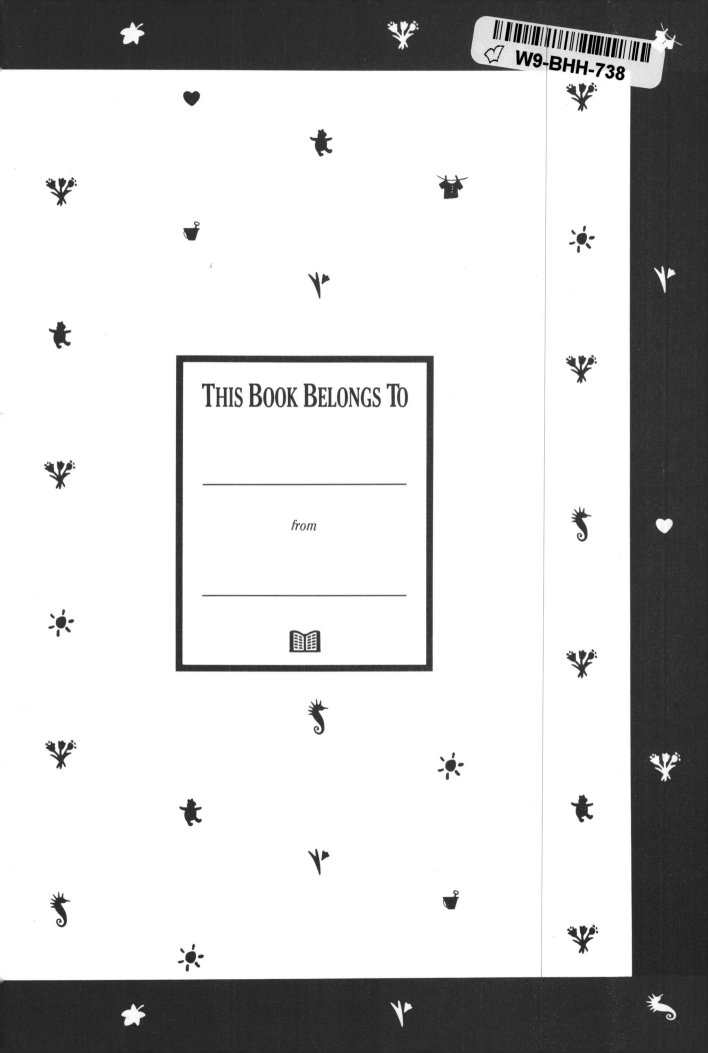

THIS BOOK BELONGS TO

_____

from

_____

ONCE UPON A TIME

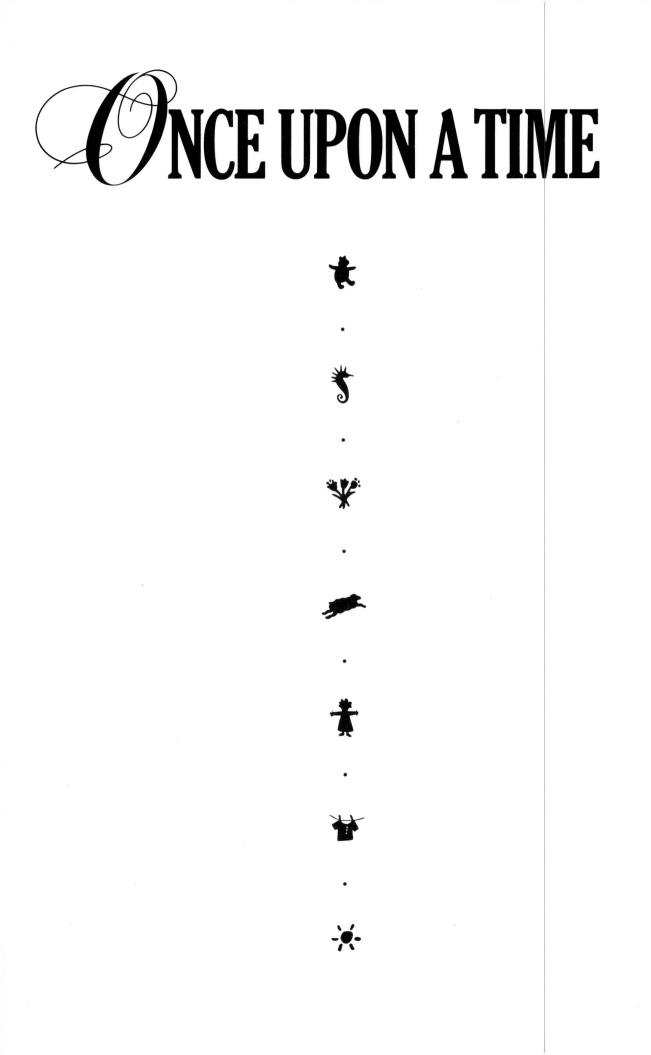

ONCE UPON A TIME

20 Bedtime Stories and Poems by
PAMELA PRINCE

Inspired by the Art of
JESSIE WILLCOX SMITH

Designed and Illustrated by
CHRISTINA DONNA

Harmony Books/New York

Published by Harmony Books, a division of Crown Publishers, Inc.,
225 Park Avenue South, New York, New York 10003, and
represented in Canada by the Canadian MANDA Group

HARMONY and colophon are trademarks of Crown Publishers, Inc.

Manufactured in Japan
Design by Christina Donna
Production Assistant: Jason Scheideman

Library of Congress Cataloging-in-Publication Data
Smith, Jessie Willcox, 1863–1935.
Once upon a time.
Summary: Twenty original stories and poems paired
with illustrations by Jessie Willcox Smith depict
children daydreaming their way around the world,
spending a rainy day in search of the biggest puddle,
and having other adventures.
1. Children's stories, American. [1. Short
stories] I. Prince, Pamela. II. Donna, Christina,
ill. III. Title.

PZ7.S651450n   1988   [E]   87-33359

ISBN 0-517-56832-2

10 9 8 7 6 5 4 3 2 1
First Edition

This Book

is dedicated

with love to

Nicholas,

Addison and

Nicole.

*Stephanie lifted a
handful of sand and let the
tiny grains sift through her fingers
like precious bits of
golden dust.*

★

TABLE OF CONTENTS

NICHOLAS, MIRANDA AND THE GOLDFISH

"Don't the goldfish look pretty?" Nicholas asked Miranda.

"Pretty tasty . . . ," thought the cat to herself. "Yes, indeed." And she licked her silky whiskers.

The boy watched as two of the baby fish darted in between the sea plants and dove toward the sand at the bottom of their miniature ocean. "I feed them all once a day," he said, "just as they told me to do at the pet shop."

"Hmmm, food . . ." Miranda's eyes glistened and she leaned toward the sparkling bowl.

"Now, listen," said Nick, tightening his hold on her. "These fish are my friends and I'm going to love and protect them, the same as I do with you. I stop Baxter when he wants to chase you up a tree, and I scared away the raccoon family when they were bullying him. If you have friends you want them to be happy and safe. And you hope that your friends will be friends with one another."

Miranda had her eye on the plumpest goldfish as he lazily circled around the bowl. Nicholas was still talking. "Please make a promise that you'll try to be friends."

She thought about how nice it was to have Nicholas for a friend. Every morning he warmed a saucer of milk for her and made sure her bowl was always full. He knew how to pet her fur softly and stroke behind her ears the way she liked. Each night she slept at the foot of his bed. He made her toys from yarn and gave her catnip on Sunday afternoons.

As the little fish swam to the surface, Miranda looked at him and then glanced up at the boy, "Oh, I'll try to be friends. I'll try. I'll try." She blinked her eyes.

The goldfish pressed his slippery nose against the window and blew out a string of frothy bubbles. And as he spun around and glided through the rippling water, Nicholas thought he saw the glistening fish flash him a grateful smile.

Miranda
had her eye
on the plumpest goldfish
as he circled around
the bowl.

SECRETS

"I have a little secret;
Please come closer, Gabrielle.
And if I share it with you,
Will you promise not to tell?"

Gabby answered, "I agree.
I'll never make a peep.
Now tell me, quick, what is the news
From others we must keep?"

Georgia whispered in her ear.
Gabrielle's eyes grew wider,
And she began to wonder if
This secret could stay inside her.

Gabby thought, "I'll just tell Sue…
(And possibly Sarah and Nell).
But when I tell them, I will make them
Promise not to tell!"

"Oh my,"
thought Gabrielle to
herself. "I just promised Georgia
that I wouldn't tell the secret
to anyone…"

🌙

KATIE CLEANS UP

This morning Katie helped Mama give Marcel, the cat, a bath. Most of the time Marcel kept his thick orange fur clean and fluffy, but yesterday he walked under the pine trees in the yard and drops of sticky sap fell onto his coat. "This chap is going to need a bath," Mama said. "Will you be my assistant, Katie?"

They eased the squirming fellow into the bathtub and rinsed him and soaped him and rinsed him again. He wriggled inside the towel while Katie rubbed and patted, but he just couldn't wait to escape. "There now, you're clean!" announced the girl as Marcel shook himself off, bolted out of the room and through the front door before she could even give him a friendly pat. "You look a little like Marcel yourself," smiled Mama. "You've got orange fur on your skirt and sweater, in your hair and all over your face!"

Just then, Katie's big brother, Michael, rushed into the room. "Hey, Katie!" he called out. "I need you to help me wash Uncle Stanley's car. You owe me a favor, remember? Come on, it'll be fun!"

And it was fun. Katie rolled up her sleeves and dipped a big sponge into a pail of soapy water. "You're closer to the ground than I am," teased her brother, "so I'd like you to wash the wheels!" Round and round she scrubbed until the muddy tires came up white and sparkling. "Now you can get the bumper," instructed Michael, as he hosed down the windows. "You know," he said, laughingly, "the car is looking great, but you're a mess!" Katie looked down at herself and chuckled. She sure was wet and dirty.

As Katie and Michael stood admiring the car, Papa drove up. He opened the door and out jumped Lucy, the dog. "Ohhh! She smells awful!" cried Katie and Michael in unison. "What happened?" "I'm afraid she got a little too close to a skunk," exclaimed Papa. "We're going to need to give her a thorough cleaning."

"Gee, I wish I could help out," said Michael, "but I've got to get going." And he took off down the street.

"That leaves you and me, Katie," said Papa. "Let's get to work."

All afternoon they set about the task of ridding Lucy of the smell of a skunk. Katie figured they washed her at least five times, and finally they sprayed her with a hint of Mama's favorite perfume. "Lucy is almost respectable again," said Papa. "She smells like lilies-of-the-valley. But, I must admit that you and I smell a bit like a skunk!"

That evening Mama said to Katie, "You've helped everyone else clean up today. Now, what would you like to do?"

"I can't wait to slip into the bathtub filled with nice warm water," replied Katie. "I want some bubble bath and a sponge and a big thick towel. And while I'm soaking I'd like you to tell me a story!"

"Your wish will be granted," answered Mama. While Katie splashed and soaped and shampooed, Mama told her a story about a household where everyone was as clean as could be, including the cat and the car and the dog. And especially the little girl who smelled just like lilies-of-the-valley when her mama tucked her into bed that night.

*"I can't wait
to slip into the bathtub
filled with nice warm water," replied Katie.
"I want some bubble bath and a sponge and
a big thick towel."*

WILL YOU BE MY VALENTINE?

*O*n the first day of school, the teacher assigned Elizabeth the desk next to Paul's. He was really annoyed. He'd hoped that he would get to sit next to his best friend, Max, and, now, he had to sit next to this girl instead. But Elizabeth gave him a nice smile, and he thought she might not be so bad after all.

The next day they had a little conversation. "What kinds of things do you like to do?" Paul asked his classmate.

"I like baseball games and animals and movies and taking walks," Elizabeth replied.

"Hey, that's what I like, too!" said Paul with some surprise.

"I got a new puppy last week," continued Elizabeth, "and he's very cute. He has blue eyes just like yours. I think I'll name him Paul!" and she laughed with a mirthful, friendly sound. Paul blushed. No one had ever named anything after him before.

When Elizabeth had trouble with spelling, Paul was happy to help her because that was his best subject. When he had trouble with arithmetic, Elizabeth was happy to help him because that was her best subject.

When he had a bad cold and stayed home in bed for a week, Elizabeth brought him his books and homework every day after school, so that he could keep up. She also took him a jar of raspberry jam she'd made, to help cheer him up. "Put lots of it on a thick piece of toast and drink some rosehips tea. You'll feel better right away," she advised.

One day during the winter they walked home from school together. It began to snow! Paul watched a snowflake land on Elizabeth's shiny chestnut-colored hair, like a star melting from the sky. Her eyes glistened with excitement as she watched the sidewalks turn a sparkling white. "She sure is pretty!" he thought to himself.

And now it's Valentine's Day. Paul spent all morning cutting a perfect heart out of thick red paper. He glued a white piece of lace onto the heart and found a Cupid's arrow made of gold foil. His big sister gave him five tiny roses made of pale pink velvet that she'd saved for a special occasion. "This is a special occasion," she said to Paul. "Go ahead and put them on the valentine. They'll look positively delightful."

Paul sealed up the valentine in a heavy envelope and put on his jacket and hat. He walked to Elizabeth's house to deliver it in person.

You can see him ringing her doorbell, can't you? Would you like to know what his valentine said?

> Dear Elizabeth,
> I'm lucky to have a new friend like you.
> Will you please be my valentine?
> Love, Paul

Paul sealed up
the Valentine in a heavy
envelope and put on his jacket and hat.
He walked to Elizabeth's house
to deliver it in person.

♥

NICOLE'S WASHING DAY

*N*icole woke up early on that Wednesday in April, threw open the window and breathed in the fresh morning air. Then, she took a good look at the two dolls next to her pillow on the bed.

"Abigail," said Nicole to the black-haired doll with rosy cheeks, "I think today would be a perfect day to wash your clothes. The sun is out and the sky is blue. It smells just like spring." Abigail looked a bit skeptical.

"Your clothes, too, Lindsay," said the girl to the smaller doll who always looked surprised and generally went along with whatever Nicole wanted to do.

After breakfast, she took her friends and a basket full of their clothes to the grassy hill behind the house. She found a big bucket and filled it with warm water. She lost track of how much soap she poured in and bubbly suds oozed up out of the pail and over the sides.

By the time Nicole started undressing the dolls she felt a little breeze creep up over the hill. Lindsay's curls fluttered. When all of the clothes were soaking in the wash tub the breeze had grown from a whisper to a shout. And by the time she started hanging all the wee garments on the line, her own apron flapped in the blustery air and her dress slapped around her legs. It took at least two clothespins to fasten even the smallest little doll sock and even the tiniest little doll blouse to the line. The miniature clothes danced with one another, arms and legs wildly moving to the music of an unexpected wind.

Nicole saw clouds crawling up behind her. Glancing up at the sky, she wondered if it might rain.

"A fine day, indeed, to wash our clothes!" complained Abigail, shivering in the cool air. The dolls didn't have anything on and Abigail felt undignified. Lindsay didn't say anything but looked even more surprised than usual.

"I'm sorry," apologized Nicole. "You just never know about April. The weather can change so fast." And she scooped up her friends, took them in the house and wrapped them up in two pieces of lovely red velvet to keep them warm. She put three cookies on a plate and made them all hot chocolate.

"I hope you'll forgive me," said Nicole to the dolls.

"We forgive you," they graciously answered. "We're having a wonderful time now, and by tomorrow morning we'll have our clothes back, fresh and clean and smelling like a fine spring day."

*The miniature clothes
danced with one another,
arms and legs wildly moving
to the music of an
unexpected wind.*

A RAINY DAY

It's starting to rain," sighed Megan. "There's just nothing fun to do when it rains. We can't take Sidney out for a walk because his fur gets all wet. We can't rollerskate or play tag in the park. We can't climb Mrs. Emmington's apple tree because it's too slippery. And I wanted to fly my new kite this afternoon. Think of all the things we can't do. Oh, it's so boring."

Devon hadn't seen her look this glum in a long time. They sat on the step and watched the sky turn cloudy.

"I'm not so sure I agree with you," he said. "Look at it this way. When it's nice out we have no reason to put on our yellow raincoats and hats and boots. Without rain we can't splash around in the streets. We can't squish around on the grass. We can't watch the geese in the garden getting a shower. And without rain we wouldn't have happy flowers and leafy trees and healthy ducks and turtles and birds and bees. Why, I'm going to get my red boat and put it in the biggest puddle I can find and pretend there's a storm at sea."

"You're just trying to cheer me up," said Megan stubbornly.

Devon continued. "You know, there are lots of good things to do inside when it rains, too—things you don't think to do unless the weather is stormy outside. We could build a secret fort underneath the dining room table. We could ask Papa to make us a fire and we could toast marshmallows in the living room. Just use your imagination!"

"Maybe you're right, after all," admitted the girl. "We can find fun things to do in any weather. Even if it's gray outside you can feel sunny yourself!"

And they sat cozily next to each other, listening to the *tap-tap-tap-tap-tap* of the raindrops falling on the giant umbrella.

"Hurry," urged Megan suddenly. "Let's get our rain gear. Let's get your boat. I want to splash along the sidewalk and get you all wet! Just think of all the things there are to do when it's raining!"

And they sat
cozily next to each other,
listening to the tap-tap-tap-tap-tap
of the raindrops falling upon the
giant umbrella.

ANNA AND THE DAISIES

A daisy for Josie,
A daisy for Nick.
A daisy for each of
my friends I shall pick.

A daisy for Megan,
A daisy for Mother,
For Grandma and Grandpa,
For Papa, another.

A daisy for Katie,
A daisy for Jen,
For Robin and Colin,
Samantha and Ben.

A daisy for you,
And I hope you'll agree,
That the meadow can spare
Just one daisy for me.

*If you
point out the daisy
you would like, Anna will be
happy to add it to her
bouquet for you.*

SANDCASTLES

As soon as Papa stopped the car, Matthew and Lily threw open the door, tore off their shoes and socks, grabbed the pail and shovel from the back seat and started running down the sandy beach to the ocean's welcoming call."Hello, Matt!"called out the first wave."Hello, Lily!"shouted the second, laughing and splashing delightfully on the shore in greeting to the children. "Hello! Hello!" they yelled back, barely able to hear their own voices above the sea spray and winds.

Lily let the bubbly white foam at the water's edge tickle her toes; Matt leaped in right up to his knees. A seagull with snow-white wings flew in lazy circles in the clear sky overhead. And a crab edged up sideways, just to keep an eye on them.

"Catch me if you can," Lily dared her brother, and took off over the sand. Matthew ran after her. They ran and ran and ran . . . they could have run forever on the endless stretch of shore. When they stopped to catch their breath, they turned around and looked for their parents. At home, Mama and Papa always seemed so big, but in the distance their parents looked like two tiny dots, and that made the children giggle.

"We left our pail and shovel with them. Maybe we can go back and make a sandcastle," suggested the boy.

When they returned, Lily patted wet sand into the pail, dreaming of towers and minarets for the sandcastle. Matt shoveled a flat place just a little ways from the water's edge, where they could begin to build. He wanted a drawbridge, a moat and a dungeon.

The castle turned out to be almost as tall as Matthew himself. In the sand he sculpted a dragon that waited to gobble up the romantic princess whom Lily imagined promenading on a balcony overlooking the sea. She found a small piece of scarlet cloth on the beach, and Matthew wrapped it around a slender piece of driftwood. He placed the tiny banner atop the highest spire of their castle where it waved gracefully in the breeze.

Every few minutes they skipped into the surf and played a good game of tag with the waves. Lily collected seashells and Matt dragged up a big piece of wet seaweed that he wanted to take home. He threw a stick into the ocean seventeen times for a friendly dog that wanted to play. And they ate the chicken and cake Mama had packed in the picnic basket.

When the sun began to set, they all piled into the car and drove home. When it was time to go to sleep, they found it hard to believe that just a few hours ago they had been on the beach, where everything glowed in the bright yellow sunshine and the sparkling blue water stretched all the way to the horizon. "We had a fine afternoon, didn't we, Lily?" asked Matthew as they drifted off to sleep, dreaming of laughing waves and snow-white birds and banners waving over golden towers.

When they returned,
Lily patted wet sand
into the pail, dreaming of towers
and minarets for the
sandcastle.

SEASHELL VOICES

I really don't understand why you have to go off on your own, Margot," Mama said, "but if you must, please don't be gone too long. Have a good time, my dear."

"I'll be fine, Mama," the little girl called out as she skipped off down the sandy shore. "I'll be back soon!"

Around the bend and over the old seawall she ran until she came to the special place. There were always wondrous shells here—starfish, conches, mussels and sand dollars. Sometimes tiny seahorses were to be found—magic little steeds that had galloped right up onto the land. Once she spied an iridescent-white gleam curving up through the sand and when the grains were brushed away she had a nautilus shell, the most graceful of all. Now it rested at home, on the shelf near her bed, where she could pick it up and peek inside at the spiralled chambers. The pearl that she'd discovered in an oyster, on another trip to the ocean, now lived beside the nautilus in her room. The two gave off a soft shine in the darkness when she awoke in the middle of the night.

But Margot mostly came here to listen. Picking up a big pale-pink cowry, she placed it to her ear and the voices began. At first she could hear only the loud rushing and roaring as the sea itself called out a grand greeting. My, it practically took her breath away every time, and she was sure the waves were shouting out her own name. But she tried to be as quiet as she could so the other sounds, more hushed, could be heard. The little girl heard some snappers snapping and squids squabbling. Way down on the bottom of the ocean floor she heard three crabs taking a walk. A whale whispered, "Well, well, well," as he watched a school of silver sardines swim by. She thought she recognized a tuna whistling a tune with a bubbling chorus. Deep beneath the surface the kelp forests swayed back and forth, and she listened to their rhythmic songs. She heard the gentle sole and the speckled trout, and the octopus was trying to say something but it was most difficult to interpret. . . .

"Margot, Margot, Margot!" she suddenly heard someone yell. But the sound was coming from somewhere else! It was her cousin, Colin, come to find her. The brown-haired girl slowly rose and tucked the speaking shell into the folds of her white muslin dress. Clutching the treasure, she ran to meet the boy who was holding something out to her in his hand. Why, it was another cowry, a brown speckled one! "Margot!" he cried out delightedly, "do you know what happens if you listen through the shells?"

Picking up
a big pale pink
cowry, Margot placed it
to her ear and the
voices began.

JUST ONE MORE BITE

"Have another bite, Ben," offered his cousin, Joanna. "It's going to help you grow up big and strong and tall."

"Will it help me grow to be as tall as Colin?" asked Ben. Colin was his big brother.

"Yes, you'll get to be as tall as he," answered the girl. "Take another bite."

"Will I grow as tall as Papa?" wondered Ben.

"I certainly think so," she said. "Another bite here . . ."

"Will I grow as tall as the grandfather clock in the hallway?" he asked.

"Maybe, if you eat enough." Joanna held up a spoonful.

". . . and as tall as the house?" Ben kept thinking.

"Who knows? Could be." said Jo, placing another bite of food in the little boy's mouth.

"And as tall as the ladder on the fire truck downtown?" Ben was getting more and more excited and more and more eager to eat.

"And as tall as the giant elm in the yard?"

"And as tall as a giraffe?"

"And as tall as a skyscraper?"

Joanna was beginning to get a little worried. She didn't want to be the one responsible for making him that tall. How would they ever find clothes to fit him or a bed big enough for him to sleep in? He wouldn't be able to fit inside the schoolhouse or ride his bicycle. It would certainly cause a lot of trouble and everyone might blame her.

"Maybe if I eat enough I'll reach the sun and moon and stars!" shouted Ben. "Give me another bite, please!"

"No," replied Joanna. "I think you've had just about enough!"

*"Have another
bite Ben," offered his
cousin Joanna. "It's going to help
you grow up big and
strong and tall."*

GRETA'S WATERCOLORS

*G*reta turned five years old just last Saturday. Grandma gave her a set of watercolors all wrapped up in purple tissue paper with a red and white polka-dot bow.

"The colors are lovely!" said the girl when she opened the box. "The yellow is like sunshine. The orange looks the same as my breakfast juice, and the pink reminds me of roses and Aunt Susannah's lipstick! I could paint a sky with the blue, trees with the greens and a little teddy bear in the forest with the browns!"

The next package she unwrapped contained three brushes with soft fur tips. Greta picked one up and tickled her little brother, Max, under his chin until he giggled.

"Now," Grandma told her, "you can create anything you can imagine. If you dream of a strawberry pie on a checkered tablecloth . . . well, you can paint it on a piece of paper. If you want to see starfish in a turquoise sea you don't have to wait until summer to go to the seashore. You can take out your new box of paints and make it come true. How about a rainbow, or a curly black poodle or a garden of daffodils? There's a whole world locked inside this little box of paints."

"I want a turtle and a chocolate chip cookie!" demanded Max.

Greta wet one of the new brushes with a dab of water and started mixing colors. The boy watched quietly as his sister made a turtle appear on the surface of the paper. She added some rocks and a river. Max picked up the brush and peered inside the tip. "Is the cookie inside here, too?" he asked. Greta and Grandma laughed as the girl painted not one, not two, not three, but twelve chocolate chip cookies. Max was impressed.

All week Greta experimented with her birthday gift. "How can I let Grandma know how much I love her and my magic paints?" she asked her mother.

"If you sit down with your watercolors," Mama answered, "I bet you'll figure out a perfect way to let Grandma know how you feel."

And so she sat down and thought and thought. "Why, of course!" she exclaimed.

Don't you think she found a perfect way to say "Thank you"?

*"If you sit down
with your watercolors,"
Mama answered, "I bet you'll figure out
a perfect way to let Grandmother
know how you feel."*

ALBERTINE IS A GREEDY CAT

Albertine's a thirsty cat,
So Chris begins to pour
A little milk into her bowl.
She meows, "More, please, more."

"You know how much I love you;
You're the cat that I adore.
But don't you think you've had enough?"
She meows, "More, more, more."

"I really think," says Christopher
(I've mentioned this before),
"That you are getting very plump,"
She meows, "More, more, more."

"I'll give you just another taste,
But then I shall ignore
Requests for even one more drop..."
She meows, "More, more, more."

At breakfast time,
Christopher pours a
saucerful of milk for his
spoiled and chubby cat,
Albertine.

ONCE UPON A TIME

Annabelle said to her brother, Jason, "Let's make up a story. Since Mama isn't here to read to us we can just invent our own."

Bob, the black-and-white terrier, barked, "Bow-wow-wow!"

"Yes, you can help us, too, Bob," answered the boy.

"Once upon a time," began Annabelle, "there was a beautiful girl named Allison who wore blue bows in her curly blond hair. She was a brave and smart person. . . ."

"But not nearly as terrific as her brother, Mason," interrupted Jason. "One day his rich Uncle Ned gave the lad a pony, all brown and white with a feathery tail. Oh, you never saw such a wonderful animal!"

"Except," woofed Bob, "for that sturdy dog, Bill, who was the best terrier in the entire world. One day . . ."

Said Annabelle, ". . . the little girl, Allison, noticed a fire breaking out in the old wood barn. She heard the pony inside."

"Lucky for everyone, Mason came along at just the right time," bragged Jason. "He knew what to do. He decided to run to the fire department and get all the people there to help."

"But Bill knew there was more he could do!" barked Bob with excitement. "He ran up the hill on the side of the barn, hopped in through a tiny window and managed to push the front door open all by himself. There was smoke! There were flames! But the pony galloped on out and he was safe! Just then, Mason returned with all the firefighters who let out a happy shout, 'Hip, hip, hooray for Bill!' "

"Hip, hip, hooray for Bill!" called out Annabelle and Jason, completely forgetting about themselves.

Bob sat and thumped his little tail. He thought it was an awfully good story.

"Hip, hip,
hooray for Bill!" called out
Annabelle and Jason, completely
forgetting about
themselves.

THE FAIRY POOL

Jennifer was the only one who knew about the fairy pool. Sooner or later she might share it with her best friend, Samantha. But right now it was her secret.

Late each afternoon, Jenny left her bedroom, crept down the stairs, tripped around the house and out the back garden, over the fence and through the big green meadow and then, following the melody of the murmuring stream, she came to the magic place.

Circled by a ring of beautiful irises was a quiet pool. The little girl knelt down and caught her breath. She watched the golden sunlight gaily dance over the deep blues and purples of the flowers, but it was the streaks of yellow nestled into the heart of each one that held her gaze. She watched the teasing fingers of the sun's rays as they tickled every blossom. The petals shimmered and gleamed and then—she tried so not to blink—right in the center of each flower, an amazing thing happened.

Silver flashes of light dazzled her eyes—she tried not even to breathe—as Jennifer saw tiny pairs of iridescent wings emerge from the ribbons of color hidden far inside the irises. The little wings beat with a fluttery whisper and announced the entrance of one, two, three, four, five dancing fairies! From every slender stem a charming creature leaped into the air, each cloaked in a single bright blue petal. Gracefully they dove from the tall blades of leaves straight down into the water. Oh, they made a delightful splash! The lily pads made perfect resting spots. The girl watched, enchanted, as the delicate sprites played, swam and frolicked.

"How lovely you are!" she cried out to them. They answered in a chorus of merry voices, like laughing bells.

And when the sun began to set, its golden fingers plucked each fairy from the water with a gentle touch, shook the jewelled drops from their hair, and tucked them back into their flower homes for the night. Silver wings vanished inside the brilliant blossoms, and the pool became smooth and hushed again.

Jenny sat for a moment in marvelous disbelief. "Who could have guessed that magic folk like these would live inside the flowers?" she wondered. "Perhaps tomorrow I really should bring Samantha!"

As she rose to leave, she softly wished the flowers good night. And they nodded and swayed and waved good-bye, with the faintest sound of laughing bells ringing through the evening air.

The little wings
beat with a fluttery whisper
and announced the entrance of one,
two, three, four, five
dancing fairies!

PLANS FOR THE DAY

Josie spooned up another warm taste of porridge from the blue-and-white Chinese bowl with the pagodas painted all around the side.

"Now, listen," she said sternly to Rupert Bear and Tiny Anita, who had joined her at breakfast, "we must discuss our plans for today. The only thing you two ever want to do is have a picnic in the garden underneath the peach tree and eat berry pie all afternoon. We've done that five times this week. I think it's time for something different, don't you?

"We could fish for minnows in the stream or walk to the park or we could make a rope swing for the big oak in the front yard. It would be fun to try out my new watercolor set and make paintings of each other in the playroom! Rupert, you could ask Stanley and Finbar over and, Anita, it's been weeks since you've seen Isabella. Why, we could all build a clubhouse under the porch or learn how to juggle or play leap frog on the lawn. We could bicycle into town, if Mama would let us, or plant some flowers or look for interesting rocks and leaves to start a collection. So, there. I've given you some suggestions. What would you like to do, Rupert?"

"I'm thinking," answered the bear.

"What about you, Anita?" asked Josie.

"I'm thinking," answered the doll.

Josie finished up her breakfast, thinking about the exciting day ahead.

"I have an idea!" piped up Anita in her small, high voice.

"Me, too!" rumbled Rupert.

"Oh, good!" the girl exclaimed. "What do you think we should do today?"

"I'd just love to have a picnic in the garden," answered the little doll, "right underneath the peach tree!"

"Sounds perfect to me," added the bear. "We could eat berry pie al-l-l-l afternoon."

"Now, listen,"
she said sternly to Rupert Bear
and Tiny Anita, who had joined her at
breakfast, "we must discuss our
plans for today."

COLIN'S VOYAGE

Colin's voyage began during the geography lesson. He closed his eyes and let the sounds of the classroom fade into the distance as his daydreams gently lifted him up and away from his desk and from his town, out of his own country and over mountaintops and vast oceans.

When Colin opened his eyes again he felt quite thrilled to see a herd of zebras rushing past, kicking up clouds of hot dry dust. And an elephant trumpeted from behind a tree as he caught a glimpse of a big white tusk flashing in the sunlight. It was very warm and when a breeze blew through the tall grasses surrounding him he felt refreshed. "I must be in Africa!" he thought with excitement. "That explains the lion sitting over there on the rock. Why, he's looking straight at me and now he's jumping off and running closer and closer. Oh! I'd better get out of here! Where can I go?"

Before he knew it he was in Paris, on a busy boulevard with many people hurrying past and speaking rapidly. He purchased a small bottle of perfume for Mama in a fancy shop. *"Merci,"* said the elegant saleslady. Then he spied the Eiffel Tower and made his way toward it. He lay on the grass underneath the tower and watched its lacy silhouette against the pale blue sky. He sighed happily. "This is a wonderful place."

"I wonder if I could go all the way around the earth to China? Perhaps I could make some other stops along the way. I want to climb a castle tower in Germany and pet a penguin in the Antarctic. I'd like to slide down a glacier in the mountains of Tibet and strum a Spanish guitar and eat Swiss chocolates. And see a Bengal tiger in India . . . from a distance."

Colin had seen many things by the time he got to China. He found himself in a village near farmlands of rice and bamboo. All the people had very dark hair and eyes and welcomed him with kindly curiosity as he wandered through the town. On tiptoe, Colin peered into the window of a small building. It was the schoolhouse. He watched the teacher point with a ruler to a map of the world. "She's giving a geography lesson!" he realized. He saw a boy in the back of the classroom just about his size and just about his age. His eyes were closed and he had a faraway smile on his face. "I wonder if he's on a voyage around the world?"

Colin's daydreaming travels came to an abrupt stop as he heard his own teacher call out his name. "Colin." The sound brought him back over thousands and thousands of miles to his desk. "Which country in the world," his teacher asked, "has the most people and the most panda bears?"

"China!" replied the boy.

"That's correct. Good work. All right, children, class is over and I'll see you tomorrow."

Colin still felt dreamy. As he slowly picked up his books to go, he gazed out the window. And, for just an instant, he thought he saw a boy just about his size and just about his age, with very dark hair and very dark eyes, peering in at him with a knowing smile.

Colin
still felt dreamy.
As he slowly picked up his
books to go, he gazed
out the window.

CHEER UP, PLEASE!

This morning Lacey lost her doll
And fell and scraped her knee.
Then she tore her favorite dress;
She's feeling sad, you see.

"Come, cheer up, please!" said David,
(He's her brother, two years older).
"I'd like to see you smile again!"
His arm went round her shoulder.

"Just yesterday I saw
That little sparrow in the tree
Look sorrowful.
Today he's warbling, joyful as can be."

David helped to comfort her
With love and kindly words;
And soon her spirits lifted
Like the wings of flying birds.

*"You'll feel
better soon, I just know
it," said David to his little sister,
Lacey, as they sat among the flowers
in the garden.*

SAMANTHA'S APPLE PIE

*S*amantha made an apple pie today, all on her own, for the very first time. She picked eight apples from Mr. Morley's tree next door. "Go ahead and take more," he offered. "In exchange, I'd love to have a piece of pie when it's done." Then she crossed the street to Mrs. Duncan's garden. The lemon tree was in full bloom, and Samantha asked if she could have one of the yellow fruits, to add a bit of tartness to her pie. "Oh, yes, go ahead, take two or three," replied Mrs. Duncan. "We'll just trade the lemons for a piece of pie when it comes out of the oven."

Earlier, Samantha had taken out her mother's cookbook to check over the recipe. "Mama, I want to bake a pie today and I'll need a few things. May I use some of your flour, salt and butter? I'll also want brown sugar and cinammon."

"Of course, my dear," answered Mama. "I'm so pleased that you're making a dessert. I have three friends coming over later, and I'll be very proud to offer them a piece of apple pie that you've made yourself." She checked in the cupboard for the ingredients. "I'm afraid we're out of brown sugar, but if you run to the corner store you can pick some up."

When old Mrs. Grant at the store heard what Samantha was up to, she exclaimed with delight, "I remember the first apple pie I ever made—must have been nearly seventy years ago. I'll make you a present of this brown sugar, but you might bring me back a little piece of that pie."

By three o'clock, Samantha had assembled everything in the kitchen. As she carefully rolled out the dough for the crust she began to wonder if there'd be any of the pie left for herself. It seemed as if it was all promised away before it was even baked.

As she put the pie in the oven, Samantha heard a knock on the back door. It was her best friend, Jennifer, and her brother, Ben. "Mrs. Duncan told us you were making an apple pie, so we thought we'd stop by to have a piece," said Jennifer. The two of them sat down and sniffed the aromas. "Sure smells good," Ben smiled.

When the pie came out it looked as perfect as a pie could look. Mama cut it into eight pieces. She and her friends each had a piece. "Delicious!" "Scrumptious!" "Fabulous!" "Wonderful!"

Mr. Morley had one. "Terrific! Must be the apples!"

Mrs. Duncan had a piece. "It's heavenly! Just the right hint of lemony tartness!"

Mrs. Grant had one. "I think it's even better than mine!"

Ben had a piece. "Yum-yum-yum-yum!"

There was one piece left. Samantha offered it to Jennifer. It was then that Jennifer noticed her friend hadn't had any of the pie that she worked so hard to make. "Don't you think we should share it, Samantha?"

So Jennifer had half a piece. "Absolutely excellent!" was her opinion.

And Samantha had half a piece. She thought it was, without doubt, the very best apple pie she'd ever tasted.

*As she carefully
rolled out the dough for
the crust, she began to wonder if
there'd be any of the pie
left for herself.*

ROBIN AND THE NAUGHTY LEAF

"If you gather up all the leaves in the garden this morning," offered Papa, "I'll take you over to the Benedict's farm this afternoon to pick out a pumpkin, and we can carve it tonight. How about it?"

Robin agreed instantly. After all, he could hardly wait to get a pumpkin to carve for Halloween. And he thought it would be great fun to rake up autumn leaves.

The dry leaves made a splendid crunching and crackling noise underfoot as the boy began to work. He stomped heartily on the pile each time it grew a bit bigger. There certainly were a lot of leaves, and soon the mound was about as tall as Robin himself.

"Come here, you," he called out to an independent little leaf. "I think you want to fly away, but you must come here and join the others." The boy scolded the fluttering leaf and tried to hook it into the rake's teeth. But the leaf had a mind of its own and just managed to slip on through. A breeze picked it up, carried it over by the tree and set it gently back down on the green grass. Its edges shook in the autumn wind and seemed to chuckle, "Catch me if you can!"

The air felt crisp and cold, but everything had such a warm color. The russet leaves curled down from the trees, sailed softly in the air and landed on the carpet of lawn below. During the summer Robin had planted chrysanthemums, and last week he noticed the scarlet, rust and yellow heads of the flowers beginning to bloom. The pumpkin farms right outside of town looked like vast oceans of big orange bubbles.

Robin looked forward to tonight. Mama planned to make some hot apple cider. Papa would build a fire, and Robin and his sister, Molly, could sit by the hearth watching the red flames lick the logs in the grate. "I'm going to carve a wickedly scary face and frighten Molly!" he thought with glee.

Lost in his daydreams, Robin hadn't noticed what that one trouble-making leaf was up to. The fellow was stirring up all the other leaves, "Come on and play! You don't want to sit around in a pile on such a fine day as this!" And with the very next gust of wind, the neatly stacked-up leaves were convinced to follow his suggestion . . . *POOF!* they went flying in all directions! And instead of only one teasing little leaf, Robin looked around and saw hundreds of them laughing and cavorting on the lawn.

The boy had to smile. "I suppose if I were a leaf I would act just the same way!" And he patiently picked up his rake again and decided to concentrate on his chore until it was done.

*The dry
leaves made a splendid
crunching and crackling noise
underfoot as the boy
began to work.*

✦

THE LOOKING-GLASS RIVER

"He was there a minute ago, I'm certain," puzzled Danny, gazing at the spot in the water where the flashing little fish had vanished. "Now I only see circles on the water and my own reflection. I wish I could see that silver minnow again; I'd try and catch him."

"And how would you catch him?" wondered Nora. "You haven't any fishing reel."

"I'd use my hands and a pinch of luck!" he replied.

She gazed at their two faces, staring back at them in the Looking-Glass River. The reflections in the water showed the fleecy clouds wandering through the sky above like sheep in a meadow on a warm summer's day . . . they didn't have to be anywhere at any time, and no one was checking up on them, just like the two children on this quiet afternoon.

Danny dipped his fingers in the cool water and jiggled them around in the middle of the sheep shapes. "Look at this, Nora! I'm tickling the clouds!" And, sure enough, the girl noticed that the fluffy white reflections wriggled around and changed their forms. "Do it again," she said and the boy danced his hand in the watery mirror, in the middle of a puffy cloud that looked like a hopping rabbit.

Nora stared and giggled as the rabbit's ears got longer and longer and finally floated away. "Here comes one," she figured, "that looks like an elegant swan. Can you tickle her under her wing?"

Just then . . . *SWOOSH!* The children heard a fine splashing sound as that mischievous minnow, who'd been hiding all along, leaped up in the air, spun around and dove back down to his cool, wet home.

"What a rascal!" the boy said, laughingly. "But, next time, you'll see. I really am going to catch him!"

"Maybe," Nora answered. "But I think you have about as much of a chance of catching that slippery fish as I do of sailing away on the swan up there in the sky."

And they both fell silent again, trailing their fingers in the Looking-Glass River, tickling the cloud creatures and dreaming of ways to make impossible things come true.

And they both fell silent
again, trailing their fingers in
the Looking-Glass River, tickling the cloud
creatures and dreaming of ways to make
impossible things come true.

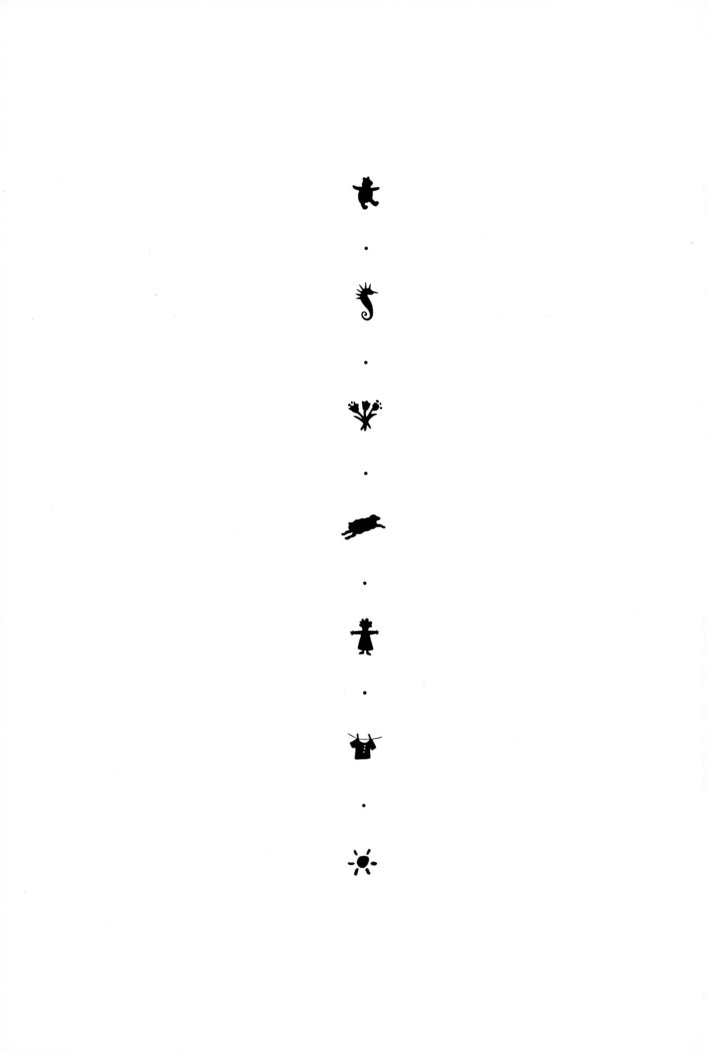